# Table of

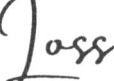

- Dear Reader — 11
- My Words Fall Out — 16
- I Stood There — 18
- My Dad — 21
- Awesome Annë: My Origin Story — 27
- To Future Awesome Annë / Awesome Reader — 32 / 33
- My Point of View — 35
- Dear Strangers — 37
- Dear College Students — 40
- Alvin — 44
- Necessary Arrangements — 51
- When the World Feels Sideways — 58
- One Day in June — 59
- Almost 50 — 61
- Mom's Story of Faith in God's Plan — 62
- This is My Last Love Letter to You — 65

## Loss

- Bingo — 69
- Diaspora — 71
- Cat's Eye — 75
- When Up is Like Down — 77
- Breakfast — 82
- Pain — 83
- One Way Ticket — 84
- Our Letter — 87
- Today — 88
- Gone — 90

# Table of Contents

## Love

- Nervous Confidence — 94
- Seen — 95
- A Door Gently Closed — 96
- My Fruit — 99
- Lost & Found — 100
- At the Social Club — 101
- Quietly — 105
- Dearest You — 107
- 3% — 110
- Their Standalone Moment — 112
- The Red Brick Wall & The Weeping Willow — 113
- Dearest Adam — 123
- Dearest Jasmine — 124
- Dearest Julia — 124
- Dearest Joy — 126
- Dearest Aaron — 127
- Cherish the Mess — 130
- I Stopped Counting — 134
- My Childhood Dream — 139
- Distance & Space in 3 Parts — 142
- Acknowledgements — 146

## Dear Annette — 149

# My Words Fall Out

## A Tapestry of Life, Loss, and Love in Letters, Poems, and Stories

### by Annë Thomas Varughese

Photography by Jasmine Dering. Art by Aaron Dering and Joy Dering

My Words Fall Out
© 2025 Annë Thomas Varughese
All rights reserved.

No part of this book may be reproduced, stored in a retrieval system, or transmitted in any form or by any means—electronic, mechanical, photocopying, recording, or otherwise—without prior written permission from the author, except for brief quotations in reviews or articles.

This is a work of creative nonfiction. Some names and identifying details have been changed to protect privacy.

Published by Annë Thomas Varughese
ISBN: 979-8-9991033-0-7

Cover design by Annë Varughese
Cover photo by Jasmine Dering
Edited by Annë Varughese and Missing Piece Solutions

For inquiries, contact: awesome.annevarughese@gmail.com

Printed in the United States of America
First Edition

*For Charlie and his baby sister.
I have always wanted to write a book for you both.*

*And especially for the five who envelope my soul.
Thank you for loving me unconditionally
despite my flaws and shortcomings.*

## Foreword by Grace Miller

One of my favorite books growing up was called "The Giver," by Lois Lowry. It's a masterfully written book that tells the story of a keeper of memories in a society that has forgotten. In the book, the Giver selects a Receiver to whom all the memories are transferred slowly, highlighting beautifully the importance of sharing the stories that create the fabric of our humanity, lest we lose touch with it.

I've had the privilege of bearing witness to the stories of Annë's life since we met more than 20 years ago. For some stories, I had a front row seat. Others, I heard through tears or laughter much later. Not every story we need to tell is easy to share, but I'm so proud of Annë's persistence in putting the words down on paper and releasing them into the world for us to receive and honor.

I hope that you enjoy getting lost in her words as much as I have, and that you are as enriched as I have been over the years by her stories.

## Foreword by Abie Gabor

I met Awesome Annë during the pandemic, at a time when connection felt distant and everything was filtered through a screen. Yet even in that virtual setting, Annë stood out. Her warmth came through immediately—welcoming, present, and genuine. You couldn't help but feel drawn to her energy.

Over the years since that first meeting, I've had the privilege of watching Annë lead with grace, serve with heart, and grow into an even more powerful version of herself. She is one of the most sincerely caring people I've ever met. Whether she's showing up for her friends, her community, or her five amazing children, Annë does so with a spirit of generosity and strength that's deeply moving. She's a servant leader in every sense—putting others before herself not out of obligation, but because it's simply who she is.

What sets Annë's writing apart is how real it is. She doesn't hide behind polished words or perfect stories. She shares with transparency, with courage, and with the kind of vulnerability that invites others to do the same. In these pages, she gives us permission to be honest about the hard stuff—and in doing so, she shows us how much power there is in owning our full story.

This book is not just a reflection of Annë's journey; it's a mirror for all of us. A reminder that we're not alone in our struggles, and that even our darkest moments can become the doorway to light, connection, and purpose.

I've been lucky enough to spend time with Annë in person as well, and I can tell you—she's as joyful and fun as she is thoughtful and wise. Her heart is as big as her laugh, and her presence makes people feel seen. You're in for a beautiful journey with this book. Let it move you. Let it challenge you. Most of all, let it remind you of the quiet strength that lives inside us all—just waiting to be shared.

## Foreword by Jouleen Dering

I've had the joy of knowing Annë for over 20 years — not just as my sister-in-law, but as someone I've shared life with through all kinds of seasons. From the chaos of raising babies to now parenting adults, I've watched her grow, evolve, and keep showing up — not just for others, but for herself.

One thing that's always stood out about Annë is how fully she feels and how freely she shares those feelings. She wears her heart on her sleeve in the best way — whether it's a moment full of joy or one full of struggle, she doesn't hide. She lets you in. In a world where so many people keep their guard up, being around her is a breath of fresh air.

Over the years, I've seen her go through so many transformations — physically, mentally, emotionally. But what I admire most is her consistent, intentional pursuit of becoming her best self. She's never settled. She's always leaning into growth, even when it's hard.

Annë has a gift with words. There's an elegance to her writing, but also a depth and realness that makes you feel like she's sitting next to you, telling the truth in love. Her voice is strong and tender all at once — and it's exactly more of what this world needs.

My hope for you, as you turn these pages, is that you feel the heart behind it. That you see yourself in her story. That you're reminded that growth is possible, that healing is ongoing, and that it's okay to show up as you are while still becoming who you're meant to be.

And to Annë — may you always remember that your worth runs deeper than you realize. You are powerful, you are needed, and your story will continue to change lives.

*"If you find it in your heart to care for somebody else, you will have succeeded."*

*- Maya Angelou*

Dear You, (yes, YOU, dear reader!)

The fact that you made the decision to open this book and read what I've written - even if it's limited to this one letter to you - is humbling.

My life story is not better or worse than anyone else's and most certainly not yours. I'd love to hear your story one day.

While you gather your thoughts and your story, this little book holds mine.

I laughed.
I cried.
I hurt others and was hurt by others.
I won.
I lost.
Some days I lived.
Other days I barely survived.

And here's where all those words - my words - fall out into this beautiful mess.

Throughout this book, I'll share a story, a poem, a letter—a glimpse into either my life or a work of fiction. Some pieces will be raw. Others will be reflective or even a little playful. But all of them carry pieces of truth.

After some pieces, there will be space for you.
To reflect. To write. To respond.
To remember what shaped you. To tell the story only you can tell.

You can use the space however you need.
Some pages may hold your laughter.
Others may catch your tears.
Some may stay blank for now—and that's okay too.

Just know:
Your story matters.
Your voice belongs here.

*Set a timer for 10 minutes, and let your thoughts spill onto the page.*

*"The essential dilemma of my life is between my deep desire to belong and my suspicion of belonging."*

- Jhumpa Lahiri, author of The Namesake

## I Stood There

I stood there in the weeds
Caught up in the lies and anger
Prickly, painful weeds
Disguised in puffs of pretty pinks.

I stood there in the weeds
Wind sweeping over me
Lifting my hair
Letting the strands fall over my eyes.

I stood there in the weeds
I let the tears stream down my face
I lift my eyes to the sun
I continue weeping.

I stood there in the weeds
I hear the crickets chirp.
I hear the songbirds sing.
I hear the rustle of the dancing weeds.

I stood there in the weeds
The sun dries my tears.
The pollen tickles my nose
I raise my arms and begin to twirl.

I dance there in the weeds.
In circles I go.

I laugh there in the weeds.
Once more before I go.

My Words Fall Out

Sometimes when I know how to answer a question or I know what to say, the words fall out of my mouth with precision and cautious delivery. But more often, I don't know the answer. I don't have the right words. I sputter and choke, and when the words fall out, they can be sharp and cut or weak and fall flat into the air.

When words are spoken to me or written down and addressed to me, I hold each word and try and feel the weight of them. But my scale is skewed and sometimes the words are heavier than intended or I feel they were flippant when the intention was far more serious.

Words fall out around me and sometimes they float softly down like snowflakes that melt into my warm skin. Sometimes they pelt on my face like rain. And yes, every now and again words fall on me in rushing angry waves, too volatile to accept, too hot to touch.

And in turn, my words can fire out of my mouth in response. It's difficult to hold the ammunition silent inside, and sometimes when I do, I am the one who gets burned.

Still, I have learned that silence is not always safe, and unspoken words can weigh just as much as the ones that fall. So regardless if they land like petals or metals, my words do need to fall out.

*What does this piece remind you of in your own life?
A person, a place, a feeling?*

*My Dad*
*This is the eulogy I gave at my father's funeral in the summer of 2023. It was one of the hardest things I've ever had to write, but also one of the most important. These are the words I shared to honor him, to remember him, and to remind myself that though he is at rest, his presence will never leave me.*

Of course, I have so many precious memories of my dad.

He was a God-fearing man.

And it's true—he was also a strict man.

But now, as a mother, I understand that much of his strictness came from a deep love for me and my brothers, from his devotion to raising us to be good people.

"Train up a child in the way he should go." That was a verse he took seriously. He knew that discipline and faithfulness to God's teachings were the foundation of a good life.

Yes, I have many memories of my daddy. But I want to share one.

This one is a core memory—a pivotal moment that shaped me into who I am today.

I was about four or five years old, standing in a living room filled with church friends after a prayer meeting. My mom was in the kitchen, chatting with the other aunties, while my dad was somewhere in the living room with the uncles, probably discussing the latest news from India. For whatever reason, I needed my dad.

I walked timidly into the living room, surrounded by tall, mustached men whose deep voices echoed around me. I went up to one of them and tugged at his pant leg. But when he turned, I realized—this wasn't my dad. I stepped back, startled. I kept looking, found another man, touched his hand, and asked, "Daddy?"

*But he wasn't my dad either.*

*Panic set in. I couldn't find him.*

*Then, suddenly, a man scooped me up and said, "Molay (daughter), I am here."*
*It was my dad. But for a split second, I didn't recognize him. That day, he had shaved off his mustache, and without it, his face looked unfamiliar. But then I looked into his eyes, and I knew. This was him.*

*And I was so glad I hadn't given up looking for him.*

*That need to find him never really left my heart.*

*So much of my life was spent searching for my dad and feeling secure when I found him.*

*I looked for him as a child, reaching for his hand as we crossed the street.*

*I looked for him at night, closing my eyes in safety as he laid his hand on my head and fervently prayed over me before I slept.*

*I looked for him in my education, in my struggles, in my victories.*

*I looked for him when I needed encouragement, when I needed prayers—for myself, for my children, for my loved ones.*

*And every time I searched for him, he was there.*

*Now, he is resting. After 81 years on this earth—he is resting.*

*But I will keep looking for him, and I know I will find him.*

I will find him in the love of our family, in the ways we continue his legacy.

I will see him in my children.

I will see him in my nieces and nephews.

I have already seen him in this church community, in the overwhelming support and love we have received.

And I will see him when I look up to the heavens. Because I believe he is there.
 Resting with his parents. Resting with our baby sister. Resting in God's peace.

It hasn't been lost on me that this mirrors the spiritual journey we are all on—the search for our Heavenly Father, the joy in finding Him, the peace in resting in Him.

One of my favorite songs expresses this beautifully. It's a song I sang for my dad when he was in the hospital a few years ago. I believe it gave him peace then, and I know it will bring me peace now. It comes from Psalm 62:

"Only in God is my soul at rest
In Him comes my salvation.
My stronghold, my Savior,
I shall not be afraid at all.
My stronghold, my Savior,
I shall not be moved."

Rest, Daddy. Rest in His peace.

*Give yourself 10 minutes to write whatever's on your mind.*

Awesome Annë: My Origin Story

I was dubbed "Awesome Annë" thanks to my success as a network marketer and entrepreneur.
It started with a simple challenge: Be awesome. Be better.
I asked myself, What does the awesome version of me look like?
And I answered:
She's awesome in her business.
She's connecting with customers.
She's reaching her goals.
She's recognized as a leader in her company.

So, I went and did the things.

One of those "things" was earning a coveted spot on a company trip to New York City when our parent company went public.
We were honored to help ring the closing bell at NASDAQ.

When they announced the winners at the company convention, I was floored. The shock was probably palpable. I remember trembling as they guided me to the mic to share some "words of wisdom" about how I had reached that milestone. I somehow stumbled my way through it, mumbling about putting my head down, working hard, and being awesome so that awesome blessings could find their way to me.

Later that night, back at the hotel room, I was washing my hands. I looked up at my reflection—and I broke down.

Who am I?
Who am I to deserve such a grand reward?
What great things have I done?
I am nothing. I am no one. This reward doesn't belong to me.
Someone made a mistake.

And I wept.

I went on that NYC trip. I basked in the energy of the city, even if a part of me still doubted I belonged there.

A few years later, life had moved on.
One day, I was driving the kids around, the radio blasting praise and worship music. We were singing and laughing together.
I pulled up to a stoplight, and Rich Mullins' voice filled the van:
"Our God is an awesome God..."

When I heard the word awesome, a thought struck me.
I remembered: I am made in His image.
If He is awesome, then shouldn't I be awesome too?

I glanced at myself in the rearview mirror and froze.
I didn't recognize the woman staring back.
I am NOT awesome, I thought.
I was in poor health. Overweight. In constant pain. Tired, struggling.

And the most heartbreaking thought came to me:
"Where did Awesome Annë go?"

Photos on social media would get tagged, and I thought surely they were mistakes.
But no—they were me.

Once again, I asked myself: What does the awesome version of me look like?

At first, I couldn't answer.
But later that day, after struggling just to walk to the mailbox, after losing my breath only minutes into a brisk walk, I found the answer:

Awesome Annë is healthier.
Awesome Annë is happier.
Awesome Annë is not out of breath.
Awesome Annë is confident.
Awesome Annë is better.

And *that* was it.
Being *better* was the awesome I was craving.

Deciding to change was hard.
Actually changing was even harder.

But I did it.
I found my confidence again.
I became the mom I wanted to be—especially for my daughter, who was battling demons of her own.

I realized something so simple and so profound:

Being better is awesome.
And I am Awesome Annë.

*Tell the story you've never told—until now.*

Dear Future Awesome Annë -

Well, look at you! You made your dreams a reality. Congratulations on your immense success of publishing your first book and be even prouder that the book made the Best Seller's List (even if it's your own "best seller's" list).

The moment you learned that your Imposter Syndrome is your Superpower, you leaned into that strength to bloom.

It's been quite the journey, and it may have seemed like there were more downs than ups. But focus on that 97%! You are resilient! You are a victor, not a victim! You are a survivor!

And what you may not have realized when you made that first step forward was that you weren't alone on this journey. So many have come alongside you and cheered you on, some were inspired by you, and even more were moved to begin their own journey to find their awesome self.

Think of this moment the next time you fix your eyes on your next goal. It may not be easy, but if anyone can do it - whatever it is - it's you. YOU ARE AWESOME ANNË.

Dear Awesome Reader,

Now, it's your turn!

Take a moment to connect with your inner awesome. Write this letter to yourself as a reminder of who you truly are, who you're becoming, and the power you hold within.

Dear AWESOME _____ [Your Name],

Today, I choose to embrace the **AWESOME** version of myself.

I am _____.

I am worthy of _____.

I am capable of _____.

I am proud of _____.

I forgive myself for _____.

I am ready to _____.

I believe in myself because _____.

I am _____ (fill in with your affirmation).

With love,

AWESOME _____
            [Your Name]

My Point of View

Walls of books circle around me and the small crowd gathered in the open space of the bookstore.

I'm here to share my book.
I'm here to speak affirmations into those who may need a light.

I read something funny.
I read something sad.
I read something real.

I look up while I read from my book.
I look into the eyes of strangers who might not really know me.
I look down at my text, voice paused.
I choose a new line to read and glance back up.
I lock eyes with a few more strangers — some from my right, a couple standing on my left.

I grasp for more words to share.
I look up and see you.
My heart jumps into my throat, my knees feel weak.

I look away, continue reading, then look back.
I look into your eyes.
I am mesmerized by your sweet, sideways grin, that dimple in your cheek.
I am drawn to your stance — one hand in your pocket, the other holding my book.
.

I force myself to look back at the last few lines, intentionally avoiding your eyes, your smile.

I finish reading.

The waves of clapping surround me, but all I can think about is you.

Thank you for coming.
Thank you for supporting me.
Thank you for encouraging me to do this.
Thank you for being my anchor in the chaos of strangers.
Thank you for seeing me.

Most of all, thank you for being you and holding on to us.
Even if it was only for a moment.

*Open letter to the man and woman we met at Jackson Square in New Orleans one very hot and sticky summer day of 2002 :*

Dear Strangers,

Yes, I'm very pregnant.
No, it's not twins.
No, you may not touch my belly.
Please do not rub my belly.
Since you touched my belly, may I rub your bald head and your big nose?

Sincerely trying to live in a bubble while pregnant,
Anne

*Write freely for 10 minutes — no rules, just you and the page.*

(Note to Reader: I was an adjunct college professor for a few years. Yes, I have said these. Too many times.)

Dear College Students,

Yes, classes will resume after Spring Break. This week-long break in the semester only marks the halfway point of the semester. It is NOT the end of the semester.

Yes, we will be reading and writing in every class period. The name of this class is Integrated Reading and Writing. I encourage you to not be surprised or upset when a chapter is assigned to read or a 3-page essay is assigned to be written. You are allowed to omit any assignments that do not require reading or writing.

Yes, it's important that you submit your own work. I'm not accusing you of plagiarizing but this text that was submitted is quite similar - almost verbatim - to an article I read online.

And no, I'm not saying this essay has been copied off of another student's essay, but the two of you should get together and decide who gets the passing grade and who gets the zero. Both identical papers can't pass.

Yes, the lessons learned here will serve you for the rest of your adult life. Reading and writing are both needed. Nay, required.

No, please do not come to class if you're sick. And please cover your mouth and nose when you sneeze. Especially when you're sneezing and coughing. And possibly hacking up a lung. No, really, go home and get some rest. Stop by urgent care on your way home.

Finally, yes, we believe in the Oxford comma in this classroom. Visualize what you're really saying when you use it and when you don't. "Come to class with your lunch, a laptop, and last night's assignment." VS "Come to class with your lunch, a laptop and last night's assignment." (Laptops and assignments do not make a nutritious meal.)

Write on!
Your professor

*Finish this sentence:*
*"If I'm honest, I still carry. . ."*

# Alvin

*(Note to reader: This was originally published in 1992 through the online magazine, Merlyn's Pen /https://merlyngrants.org/teen-writers/ Vol. 8, Issue 1 / October/November 1992)*

Ever since the day I pushed my older brother off MY toy horse and he broke his head, I have always yearned for a sister. At that time, it was just the two of us: Abraham vs. Annë. He was only one year older than I, and we did virtually everything together. Especially fight. We played cars together and we ended up fighting over whose car was fastest. We watched TV together and we ended up fighting over whether or not Big Bird could really fly.

Yes, we did everything together, and every moment we shared always resulted in another outbreak of World War III. It's not that I hate my brother. Honest. I love him just as much as I love broccoli. I really do not hate my brother! I just dislike him very much.

But whatever we did, and whatever fight we got into, I was always at a disadvantage. "Little girls are to treat their older brothers with respect" is a quote my mom says comes from *The Mother's Almanac of Raising Little Girls,* volume 18, section 42, page 3691, paragraph 2c. Yeah, right. I know there is no such book because when I was six, I leaned what white lies were. And that's exactly what my own mother was telling me: a white lie. Anyway, Abraham always got away with our bickering while I got left with the blame. And they say the youngest child gets all the breaks. Ha. Ha. Ha. Because of these continuous mistreatments, I hated (I mean "disliked") my brother more and more. And the more I disliked him, the more I wanted a sister.

I used to dream about my sister. She would look just like my Betsy Wetsy doll: golden locks and soft white skin. In April or May of 1983, when I was eight years old, my mother made the most important announcement of the year. She was going to have a baby! Boy, was I excited!

The only problem was I knew I was going to get a sister sooner or later, and I wanted to see her *right then*. But my mother explained to me about the facts of life and that there was just the same likelihood for the baby to be a boy. But I did not want a boy! And of course, you know who wanted a brother! Abraham wanted a brother just so they could start a clan or a gang or something and throw me out. But no way, José, was I about to get thrown out of my own house because of a couple of boys; I had to somehow get my sister. So I prayed.

This idea did not come to me until after the pastor had mentioned the power of prayer one Sunday morning. I prayed for a sister in the morning after getting out of bed. I prayed for a sister before eating breakfast. I prayed for a sister before I ate my lunch. I prayed for a sister before and after eating dinner. I prayed for a sister before going to bed. Six times a day I prayed for a sister. Every day.

First I would pray for Mommy and Daddy. Then, if I was in a good mood, maybe Abraham. Finally I would pause and pray in my mind for a sister. "Lord, you just gotta give me a sister—you just gotta!" Six times a day, every day, until August 16. I would not pray out loud for fear that if my brother heard me praying for a girl, he would also pray for a boy and God would listen to him (because he's older than I) instead of me and give us a boy.

On August 16, right before lunch, my mom decided it was time. My dad was at work so my uncle came and took Mommy to the hospital and Abraham and me to the local day care. That evening, after a long day at the nursery, Daddy came to take us to see Mommy.

And Alvin.

Alvin! Of all the names in the book, they could only find the dumbest! I was not mad. Honest. I was FURIOUS!!! A boy! "'Noble friend, loved by all,'" gloated my dad to all our friends when he called to announce the birth of the baby. Yeah, sure— loved by all except me.

On that sunny summer day, when we came home from the hospital, an air conditioner technician was working on the A/C unit. He thought it was hilarious the way I was crying and shouting about how I hated the new baby. But not after I kicked him. And right where it counts. (Hey, it's not my fault he wasn't ready.)

Whenever I looked back on that day, I wondered if I was the only person who could ever get so jealous and hate a baby like Alvin. The wondering stopped five years later in 1987 when my mother made the most important announcement of my life. She was going to have a baby!

Boy, was I excited! And boy, was Alvin excited also. He wanted a brother and he wanted one then. I, on the other hand, had plenty of patience to spare. I also had plenty of wisdom from my previous experience. I did not have to worry about praying quietly, because now I wanted Alvin and Abraham to hear. I also did not have to ask God for a sister; I thanked Him for giving us one. Every day I prayed until November 16.

Monday, November 16, when I came home from school, Abraham told me Mom was at the hospital and Dad was with her. When Alvin came home from school, I passed the news on to him.

Later, Dad came home from the hospital, saying it was not time yet, and then returned with Alvin. At 6:00, Dad called and announced the birth of—MY NEW SISTER!!!

A girl!! And they named her Annette! After ME! But my joy did not last long, because Alvin kicked me.

*Write your own poem, letter, or story, starting with the line:
"I remember..." or "There was a day when..."*

# Necessary Arrangements (Part 1)

One weekend during my junior year of college, my parents discovered two unfathomable truths about my young adult life. First, I was dating. Second, he was outside our race. It didn't matter that he was a smart, handsome fellow I met in my advanced physics class. I went behind their backs, and they were devastated, betrayed, and furious.

My parents, immigrants from India, had meticulously planned my life to be traditional from the moment I was born in America. I grew up blindly obeying them—until I discovered something untraditional: autonomy. I longed to assert myself, but each attempt was swiftly crushed. I led a double life—publicly following the path they created for me while secretly trying to live my truth.

The most egregious of my untraditional desires? To be social. To date. My parents expected me to stay home and study until they arranged my marriage. When they found out about my first college romance, they erupted. They forbade me from continuing the relationship, threatening to pull me out of school. I told them I would rather leave their home than leave him. In return, they resorted to threats and demands, their anger twisting into desperate prayers that I repent.

I stopped arguing and started hiding again. I let them believe the relationship had ended. I built a bubble of love around myself, blocking out their noise.

Then summer came, and he went home across the country. Before he left, he suggested we stop hiding. He didn't understand (or didn't want to understand) the repercussions. My world was foreign to him.

I lived in an emotional cage built by cultural traditions and strict parents. Still, I agreed and told my parents.

As expected, it was a disaster. My dad intercepted his letters. My mom answered his calls with hysterical shouts in a language he didn't know. His gifts were sent back, unopened.

And then—he stopped.

A week after his last failed attempt to reach me, he showed up unannounced at the department store where I worked. I was thrilled to see him—too thrilled to notice his aloofness. When I reached for his hand, he jerked away. Our bubble deflated. At the food court, over Taco Bell, he ended our relationship.

I tried to walk away, but he caught up with me. His friend had dropped him off; he needed a ride home. My inexperienced heart was too broken to tell him no. Instead, I arranged a ride for him, and then I went home. I told no one about what happened. I cried myself to sleep. One tearful night turned into a month of tearful nights.

I knew my parents would be thrilled, so I waited before telling them. When I did, my mother jumped up and yelled, "Hallelujah! The chains are broken!" My father stormed into my room and shoved every gift and keepsake from the relationship into a small box. He bent and broke things to make them fit. Then, he mailed it all back. I wasn't sure if he was punishing my ex or punishing me.

The next month passed in a fog. My mother, seeing my heartbreak, softened. One night, she sat on my bed and gently asked if Daddy could help—by arranging a marriage. I was sad enough to oblige.

# Necessary Arrangements, Part 2
## The Arrangement

On a rainy Saturday morning, the doorbell rang. A young man, his family, and other strangers entered our home. My mother and aunts kept me in the kitchen, where I could hear stiff greetings in Malayalam as my father ushered them into the formal living room.

When it was time to make my appearance, I nervously tugged at the pallu of my pink sari, my fingers heavy with anxiety. My mother handed me a tray of china teacups filled with chai. Before I stepped out, my aunt whispered, *Lower your eyes. Serve with your right hand. Move quickly. Don't speak.*

"Oh, and don't trip on the sari," I thought.

The china clinked softly as I shuffled into the overcrowded room. Men filled the couches around the coffee table. Women sat on extra chairs squeezed into every available space. I served chai to the elder men first, then the women. The young man who had come to meet me sat tall, his eyes quietly observing.

The meeting had been arranged because my father had told his brother I was "of age." His requirements were simple: my husband must be filled with the Holy Spirit, preferably a pastor, well-educated (a graduate degree was ideal), and tall.

Well, the man in front of me was tall.

At my father's request, my elder brother took us to the family room to "get acquainted." I nearly laughed at the idea that I was about to meet my potential husband for the first time—minutes before possibly agreeing to marry him.

He was friendly, with a kind smile. He was impressed that I sang in the worship team and played piano. I was impressed that he had traveled from India to Saudi Arabia to America. He was thrilled that I was born in the States.

Then he said he wanted to return to India indefinitely to preach.

I had only visited India once as a child. I worried about leaving my family behind, about living in a foreign land. He didn't. But he was happy that I could be a female lead vocalist for his evangelizing Christian band.

As the evening ended, I braced myself for my relatives' barrage of teasing and questions. They insisted it was a match. It wasn't.

Necessary Arrangements, Part 3<br>The Decision

When I finally sat alone with my parents, I voiced my concerns. He had practically asked me to audition for his band. I wanted love; he wanted a lead singer.

For the first time, they listened. The proposal was called off.

Later, I learned he married someone else for a green card. I laughed at the revelation. Had any part of that arrangement been sincere? Or had it all been a ruse?

A month later, as I packed for college, I looked around my empty bedroom, surrounded by large plastic containers stuffed with my clothes—T-shirts, skirts, blouses, even sarees. Everything that embodied who I was.

And I knew.

I didn't belong in this house anymore. Maybe I never had.

These walls had witnessed my struggles as a first-generation Indian woman, torn between two worlds. I longed to return to school—to a life where my choices were my own. As I loaded the van, a wave of boldness washed over me.

I was done living by arrangements.

From now on, any and all future arrangements would be made by me, for me.

No one else.

*Do a quick 10-minute writing sprint. No editing. Just go.*

When the World Feels Sideways

When the world feels sideways,
and I think I'm about to fall over,
I remember
to engage my core,
making sure my feet are firmly planted,
roots digging deeper into the ground.
But sometimes, I still stumble
or trip.

Sometimes, I fall sideways, too.
Dizzy, confused, lightheaded—
I need to sit,
put my head in my hands,
take breaths, slow and steady.

My mind may spin,
but I know the spinning will stop.
With arms outstretched, I rise again,
the world still sideways,
knees weak, legs wobbly,
but I try.

When the world feels sideways,
I take a moment to decide—
Will I laugh and fall, too?
Or rise with strength
to fight that falling feeling?

One Day In June

We sit outside
under the shade of the oak tree
trying to escape the baking sun
but our efforts are in vain.
Sticky
sweaty
we melt in the humid heat.

We sit outside
under the shade of the oak tree
and sip on tepid lemonade.
The sun slowly retreats behind the horizon
changing the skies from
blue to orange to pink to
a deep, sleepy purple.
Fireflies flitter carelessly
in the warm, thick air
while the familiar smell
of cut grass
lingers around us.

It's too hot to think
too hot to sleep
too hot to do anything..

We try and enjoy
the rest of my day
by indulging in cherry flavored popsicles
and the warmth of the June sun
embraces our cold treats.
The red juice from my popsicle
races down my fingers
and I smile.
I am one
sticky
sweaty
and happy
birthday girl.

*Share your favorite (or worst) birthday story.*

Almost 50.

It's a weird notion, honestly. With all the death I've experienced in my life, I can honestly say I didn't think I'd live to see 50. But now that I'm here, I realize I don't *FEEL* 50. I feel much younger. I mean, don't get me wrong - I do have an achy body and forgetful mind. My eyesight won't let me forget my age...

But I don't feel like what I thought a 50-year-old woman would / should feel like.

I've been carrying a lot of excess weight for most of my adult life. For a hot second, I was slender and full of desire - like I was when I was in college. But then I found myself putting down the salad fork and picking up an old-fashioned donut. Or a Nutella-filled 'uncrustable'. Or a Nutella-filled 'uncrustable' smothered and drenched in cinnamon sugar..

I ate my way through the dark shadows of my failing marriage. I ate my way through the grief of my daddy's death. I ate my way through the carnage of our divorce.

I ate and ate and ate. I realized today that through all that grief, sadness, and depression, I just wanted to steal a moment of joy. And when I rediscovered it in food, I wanted to get that delicious dopamine high.

Until I realized I ate my way into 2025 - the year I turn 50.

What will this year bring? I've been fighting for so long to get out of survival mode. Now I've put myself in a self-made survival mode, and I'm trying to crawl my way out. And if anyone can do it, it's me, Awesome Annë.

Mom's Story of Faith in God's Plan

My mother, Annamma Varkey, is living proof of God's faithfulness and the power of unwavering faith in His plan. Her journey as an immigrant and a nurse is one of courage, resilience, and deep trust in God's guidance.

It seems so unfathomable to me that in 1968, she arrived in the United States with just seven dollars in her pocket, sponsored by Parkland Memorial Hospital in Dallas. She often recalls the excitement of eating her first meal at the hospital cafeteria, a moment that marked the beginning of a new chapter in her life. When she recollects that moment, the energy in the room shifts, and the memory is almost palpable.

The road for her in this foreign land wasn't easy—she faced ridicule because of her accent and struggled with the challenges of adapting to a new country.

But my mother never let hardship define her. She prayed through every difficulty, and with God's grace, she found opportunities to further her education, strengthen her nursing career, and overcome the language barriers that once held her back. She believed that God had placed her on this path for a reason, and she walked it with faith and determination.

In 1972, my father, Thomas Varughese, joined her in the U.S., and together they built a life in a suburban Dallas town, choosing the town for its strong educational opportunities for their four children—my brothers, Abraham and Alvin, my baby sister, Annette, and me. My parents prayed over every decision, seeking God's direction, and their faith led them to a life filled with blessings and success.

With her unwavering work ethic, mom devoted her energy into her career. Nursing was never just a job for my mother—it was her calling. She poured her heart into caring for her patients and their families, always treating them with the same kindness and mercy that God had shown her. She wanted to be more than a nurse; she wanted to be a source of comfort, healing, and grace. Whether mentoring new nurses, writing training guides, or working to improve hospital processes, she dedicated herself to serving others in a way that reflected her faith.

Even when she went through unimaginable pain, her faith remained her strong foundation. In 1989, our family was utterly devastated at the sudden death of our sweet Annette. It was a tragic car accident that shook us all. As we leaned into each other for comfort, I remember my mother set the example for us to seek God's peace for the blessing of His comfort.

Over the course of forty-one years, my mother worked in some of the most demanding medical environments—sixteen and a half years in the Parkland Emergency Room, ten years at Children's Medical Center, and over fourteen years at the VA Medical Center in Dallas. Her dedication and excellence were recognized with numerous honors, including the Unsung Heroes and Heroines award in 1999 and being named one of the Great 100 Nurses in 2000. She also authored multiple guides for student nurses and developed dosage charts for RNs, always striving to leave the nursing field better than she found it. But she never sought recognition—every achievement, every accolade, she credited to God's blessings.

My mother's faith has shaped every part of her life. It gave her the strength to leave behind the familiarity of her home in India and build a new life in a foreign land. It gave her the courage to stand firm in the face of adversity.

It guided her in raising her children, serving her community, and dedicating over fifty-one years to mission work. Through it all, she has remained steadfast, always trusting that God's plan was greater than her own.

I hope her testimony demonstrates my way to honor the sacrifices and triumphs of my beautiful mother—an immigrant nurse, a women who took a leap of faith into the unknown and built legacies that will inspire generations to come. I am so proud of my mother and grateful for the chance to share her story.

She has always said that everything she has done is because of God's grace. I know that from that grace she drew her strength, her kindness, and her unwavering faith.

And I must believe that that same grace is in me, too.

This is My Last Love Letter to You

Dear You,

It wasn't supposed to be like this.
We made plans — grand plans wrapped in hope and blanketed in prayers. We dreamed aloud of what we could build together, what we might accomplish.

But I don't think we ever truly woke up from those dreams.
I'm just as guilty, and you know that. We spent beyond our means, never earning enough to sustain the life we imagined. And what we overspent, wasn't money, but time. We were blessed to raise five incredible humans, yet we struggled to give them the blessings they deserved.

The love I had for you still lingers, quiet and unchanged. But the desire to share space, to share life—that part has faded.
We both know that when we knelt at the altar all those years ago, we never imagined our life together would fall apart.

Still, joy comes in its own quiet way. We may have wept through many nights, but joy—like scripture promises—did come with the morning. It's a joy to hear the kids laugh about their times and memories with you. It's a joy to see them carry the virtues we once taught side by side.

Even though our forever became never,
You—and all that we were—will always be a permanent blessing in my soul.

Me

P.S. Happy Anniversary of when we started our family.

*Revisit a moment when you had to let go—of something or someone. What did that create space for?*

# Loss

"No one ever told me that grief felt so like fear."

- C.S. Lewis, author of The Chronicles of Narnia

Bingo

What's on your bingo card?

Rainbow streamers on my bike
Fell down
Skinned my knees
Broke a bone
Bright blue bandaids
Got back up

Trapper Keepers
Scratch n Sniff Stickers
Notes passed with my name on them
Some with truths
Others with lies
Cried in bed

Grew taller
Got wiser
Noticed boys
Noticing me
Tripped and fell

Brushed myself off
Wrote term papers
Had late night study sessions
Overslept
Rushed to class
Passed that crush
Crushes turned to crushed.

Fell in love
Walked down the aisle
Moved out of state

Had a baby
Moved out of state again
Had two more

Went on car rides and plane trips
Earned one degree
Two degrees
Never finished the third
Moved out of state again

Had the last two babies
Found a job
Quit
Found another job
Got laid off
Bank was full
Bank bounced
Fell and rose again

Taught
Learned
Grew
Moved
Loved
Went through Death
And then a Divorce
Fell
Stood

Full Card.
Bingo..

Still standing.

Diaspora

I am an orphan with parents.
At least, some days I feel this way.

I belong here, but I don't.
I speak this language and understand another.
And sometimes I feel lost in every translation.

I am not white,
but sometimes I forget.
Surrounded by Caucasian faces,
my own brown reflection blurs.

I am not just a Malayalee,
but the weight of a sari
feels like borrowed silk,
as if I am only playing a part.

At family gatherings,
voices roll like waves in a language
I understand but cannot swim in.
I smile, I nod,
but the words slip through my fingers.

Indian elephants,
carved out of sandalwood,
line the mantle of my heart—
silent, unmoving,
carrying stories I do not fully know
but cannot bear to forget.

Pizza on one day, biryani the next—
but taste alone does not make roots.
One world raised me,
the other made me.
And yet, I do not fully belong to either.

I feel like an orphan,
not of blood,
not of home,
but in life.
I exist in between,
everywhere
and nowhere
all at once.

*Write about a time when you felt a specific emotion.*
*[For example: free, stuck, brave, broken, seen].*

Cat's Eye

Golden curls
donned the head
of the child under
the dancing branches of the weeping willow.

His pudgy fists
are busy
digging deep into
the pockets of his
red corduroy overalls
searching for
his prized cat's eye.

Frustrated,
he whispers a lisped
"Where is it?"
and wipes the dirt
from his cheek.

He tries again–
plunging both fat fists
deeper into the pockets
of his red corduroy overalls
searching
for that shiny cat's eye.

But as the sun falls
behind the weeping willow
his pockets reveal their secret.

A tear rolls down
his rosy pink cheek
as one hand pulls out
three dirty stones
and the other hand finds
a hole.

## When Up is Like Down

Up is like down when upside down –

when your red balloon pops

or worse

when it escapes from your hand

searching for freedom across oceans with the clouds.

When the sun sets and the moon rises,

it's a quiet joy or a happy sad.

You may be happy but then a shadow falls on you

and you realize you're not really happy, but not sad,

either.

You're on the verge of falling into a depression

but you can almost feel a giggle tickle up inside.

Up is like down when you buy

deliciously beautiful white roses

trimmed with innocent white daisies.

A bouquet so elegant

you ache to take in another deep breath and

fill your soul with the sweet smell of their life.

But before you exhale you taste the bitter reminder

that you bought them to lay on your baby sister's grave.

Up is like down when while you cry over her tombstone
you taste your salty tears melting into the short sweetness
of her sixteen month old laugh.

You smile inside your tears as you remember how
your sister loved to live,
to learn, to play, to sing, to dance,
to call your name.
But as soon as you laugh at those memories,
you remember with a cold sadness that
she also loved her new talent of walking and
she had just ventured out to explore beyond the open back door
when daddy pulled the van out of the garage.

Up is like down when you long to turn back time
and run ahead of her to shut that back door or hold her
for one second longer so she couldn't walk away.

Or when you long to feel her weight
in your arms again while she sleeps
and you wish you never knew the weight
of touching a tombstone so small.

*Have you ever experienced something similar?*
*How did it shape you?*

Breakfast

Warm in my plaid flannel pajamas
(a gift from you last Christmas)
I watch my world collapse.
I call out for your comforting arms
and together under your grandmother's quilt
 we cry over the innocence shattered
by two planes.

The morning sun tries to melt away our fears
but the poison of hate has killed my solitude.

Watching the world in pain leaves a bitter taste
in my heart.
I choke on my dry toast and leave my cereal to soak in milk
while I return to bed.

I drown my
 nightmares
 in my dreams.

Pain

I cry when I get
those paper cuts
and grimace at the little
kitten's claw scratches.

I hate carpet burns
and those scraped up knees
scar my memories.
Static shock from a
wooly sock jolts me wide awake.

Don't you hate it when a
fingernail is cut too close?
Or when you
step on a thorn,
a shard of glass,
a needle hidden in the carpet?

Bleed
Cry
Kiss
Hug
Put on a Band-Aid
with Elmo,
Strawberry Shortcake,
or even Spiderman
to ease the pain.

But how do you soothe
my broken heart?

One Way Ticket

The wind and the leaves waltz around us
as the conductor bellows his final warning.
Another train rushes forward to follow the setting sun.
You turn to look at me, but I look away.
Fear grips my heart as I watch a blond child
take measured steps to someone's lost ticket.
He sees my eyes, laughs, and the impish creature
scurries away.


I lean into you asking for one more taste.
The scent of jasmine begs for attention
but I draw in another breath of you,
smelling your lips, your life.
The wind grabs my red scarf and
indulges me in a game of catch, but instead
I grab your hand once again.
I look into your eyes and
beg you not to leave.


But the train whistles my nightmare,
and it echoes around me and then in me
as I stand alone,
tasting the end of our beginning,
the bittersweet beginning of our end.

*Reflect on a moment of loss or letting go. Or write a letter to the person or version of yourself you released.*

Our Letter

*(Note to reader: This was a college assignment. In my mind, I imagined how news may have traveled before modern technology.)*

The sharp, cold air
seeps its snowless breath
through the brick walls,
invading my world and
closing itself around my pen,
stinging me so sharply,
my entire body
quivers at its torture.
The clock announces
the arrival of midnight.
Together we sit behind
the strong, mahogany desk,
my love and I,
staring
at the mocking white flames
trapped in the furnace.
Before us, on the desk,
lingers
a letter barely touched,
addressed to our parents.
The white paper waits
as empty as our souls
have become
since the evening of
our baby's death,
two nights before.

Today

I think today I'll run outside
and let the wind comb my hair.

Do you want to come?

We'll run to the park,
skip in the grass and
I'll race you to the swings.
I want to fly high,
reach up and touch the sky.
If I can't touch the clouds,
then I'll dive back faster
and swing up higher
and I'll try again.

Let's climb the monkey bars
or fly a kite
or sit on a thick branch of the maple tree
in the park
and pretend to be king and queen.

We'll have a royal lunch of
peanut butter and jelly sandwiches
and quench our thirst with
delicious grape Kool-Aid.
I even packed some M&Ms
in my Snoopy lunchbox.

On this sweet summer day
we only have to worry about
scrapes on our knees,
finding a home for ladybugs and fireflies,
and following the rules
in another game of tag.

We won't waste a moment
thinking about
the taxes we owe,
the pile of bills on our desk,
the balding tires of our worn out car,
the broken sink,
or your lost job.

Gone

I touch the cotton candy to my tongue
and delight in the painful sweetness
as it melts into nothing in my mouth.

I stretch my hand to the sky
and catch a fat, fluffy snowflake,
watching in wonder
as it melts into nothing in my hand.

I tip my toe in the water and swirl it around,
laughing as the splash surprises me —
then sighing
as the ripples melt into a calm nothing.

I light the wick of your candle,
the sharp burnt smell stings my eyes
while my breath snuffs out the flame
and it melts into a smoky nothing.

I gently open my heart,
hold your love inside me,
and I whisper goodbye
as you melt into the nothing of tomorrow without me.

*Write about someone or something you loved and had to let go. What would you say to them now, if you could?*

*"You can't deny you ever loved them, love them still, even if loving them causes you pain."*

*- Judy Blume, author of Summer Sisters*

Nervous Confidence

Hi.

Sometimes that word is a simple greeting.
Bold.
Friendly.
Contagious.
But not this time.

This time it means I'm still nervous around you.
This time it means I'm drawn to you.
This time it means I feel that spark between us.
This time it means I love looking into your eyes.
This time it means I want to be flooded with your laughter.
This time it means I'm smitten when you touch me.
This time it means I long to linger in your embrace.
This time it means I want so much more of you.
This time it means I really like you.

And when you say Hi back,
It means I feel seen.
It means I feel your desire.
It means I believe you like me, too.

Hi.

Seen

The last time I felt truly seen
was many yesterdays ago.
Right now, I feel like I'm hiding in public—
out in the open, but does anyone really see me?

I go to work,
I succeed,
I stumble.
I am encouraged, and I am praised.
But the moment I shut my computer,
I'm alone in my home.
Even when the kids are here,
I'm alone.

I go to church,
I lift my face to the heavens,
I shake hands with others.
But the moment I leave the sanctuary,
I'm alone In the crowds of people
who are all heading out the exits.

I miss connections.
I miss physical touch.
I miss intimacy.

The last time I felt truly seen
was too many yesterdays ago.

Far too many to count.

A Door Gently Closed: Choosing Peace Over Potential

To whom it may concern

I do appreciate the introduction
and the friendly banter.

I did rather enjoy the silly exchange we shared
and the deep dive into where our faith has taken us
and how our faith brought us here.

It took a second,
but I'm now okay that the spark blew out.

If you're interested, I won't have to wonder.
If I am reaching out, that just means you're not leading.
My peace is far more important than
anyone's potential.
And, for what it's worth
- and I am worth a lot -
I don't chase.
I choose.

Today I choose me.
I choose to release anything that does not serve me.
I choose to rest in my worth,
Not in your response or lack thereof.

Tomorrow,
And every day after,
I rise refreshed, radiant, and very ready.
Because I know and believe:
I am already enough.

*Create a snapshot scene from your own story.
Where are you? Who is there? What happens next?*

My Fruit

The sun hides behind gray clouds as I walk into the grocery store.
I select a rusting cart and steer its unstable wheels around the
lemons past the grapefruits to the bananas.
A woman with long silver curls,
too much jewelry, and a bright blue scarf smiles shyly
and moves aside to let me carefully avoid
a banana bunch with spots and choose some still ripe and green.
I check my list again and after selecting two sweet mangos
I leave the produce department for some creamy frozen yogurt
and then, I walk to the counter.
I hand the cashier a twenty, and I put the change in my back
pocket while she bags my groceries.
I head out the door to my silver Honda, and I can't help but skip
to the song stuck in my head.
The smile on my face just can't be erased.
With my eyes up to heaven, I blush in wonder and excitement
once again that
I am finally pregnant.

Lost & Found

I feel lost, and I want to be found. Who am I?

I want to be me, but I don't know how to do that.
What does that even mean?
What does that even look like? Who am I?

I want to be me, but I don't know who I am.
I don't know how to be me.
I don't know how to just be.

I want to be me, but I don't feel like I exist.
I don't feel like I belong.
I don't know what I even want.

I want to be me, but I don't know how.
Maybe I am not lost— maybe I'm just waiting
for me to stop disappearing into everyone else.

Maybe the first step is letting myself be confused,
and letting that be okay.
Maybe I'm scared that when I finally meet me,
I won't be enough.

Maybe finding me isn't a straight line—
maybe it's a slow unfolding, like petals opening
only when they feel the sun.

I don't have all the answers, but I know this much:
I'm tired of disappearing. I'm ready to begin.

And maybe—just maybe— admitting that
is the first step in finding me.

At the Social Club

She parked, and when she got out, she saw him standing by the door of the club, waiting for her. She smiled as she waved and extended an arm for a quick side hug.

They walked in together, and he pulled out a chair for her at a table of his friends. Introductions were made—loud and friendly—and she felt herself relax into her seat, smiling.

She sat next to him, watching the way he leaned in, his tall frame relaxed yet somehow alert. His bright blue eyes seemed to glow in the dim light. His slender fingers, strong and kind, reached out beneath the table, brushing her wrist gently. No one else saw the touch, hidden from the world.

Her breath caught, a soft shiver running down her spine. She leaned in closer, the scent of him wrapping around her like a whisper. She could feel the familiar flutter of nervousness, even now, sitting so close.

They engaged in the conversations that swirled around them. The room echoed with loud laughs, clinking glasses, noisy silverware, and blaring TVs. But she was focused on something else. She was focused on someone else.

After about an hour of friendly banter, he leaned over and quietly asked if she was ready to head out. She nodded, and they gave their hugs and said their goodbyes. They walked out of the room with space between them, careful and quiet.

Outside, their steps were separate, yet somehow together. She knew his friends were watching—wondering, maybe, about the subtle shift in their connection.

She wanted to reach for his hand, but she wasn't ready to share what was still private, still hers. Not yet. Not with them. She sat in her car for a few moments, basking in their unspoken spark.

*Recall the first time you fell in love—whether it lasted or not. What do you remember about how it felt, and who you were then?*

Quietly

Loving quietly can be peaceful
It can also be painful
I miss the sound of your voice
I long to hear your laughter.
Are you loving quietly, too?

Laughing quietly fills a soft spot in my heart.
It also reminds me of who I'm missing -
the one whose voice I want to hear laughing.
The one I hope wants to laugh with me.
Are you laughing quietly, too?

Hoping quietly brings me strength
I can hold on to what might be possible.
It also releases a silent fear
That my desire to share life with you may never come to exist.
Are you hoping quietly, too?

Living quietly rushes my soul
I feel like flying when I live like that.
I also feel like I'm falling and failing
And I might lose the joy in my smile.
Are you living quietly, too?

Smiling quietly is like a well-kept secret
Something sweet and delicious.
It's also bittersweet when I can't see you
smile back. So I cry.
Are you smiling quietly, too?

Crying quietly sometimes heals me
My heart might be slowly breaking
Inside my life is a dull pain, a dull noise,
A dull ache.
Are you crying quietly, too?

Aching quietly sometimes
Wakes me up from what hurts.
Helps me remember to feel again
Sometimes it heals my love for you.
Are you aching quietly, too?

Loving quietly can be peaceful
And painful at the same time.

Are you loving quietly, too?

Dearest You -

Thank you for loving me in my darkest moments. Thank you for holding me close and helping me feel protected. Thank you for teaching me what it means to be seen, to be heard, to be loved.

Thank you for being there to guide me back into the light. Thank you for never leaving my side, especially when I may have pushed you away. Thank you for holding me ever closer.

I don't know if I could ever be a friend like that back to you. I don't even know how to start. But watching you and loving you is inspiring me to be better.

I love you.

*Take 10 minutes to breathe and write what's stirring inside.*

3%

What Perfectionism Taught Me About Being Enough

"What happened to the 3%? Why is it missing?"
That question echoed through my childhood every time I came home with a 97%.

It happened often—especially in math, history, sometimes science. I tried hard to retain that information. I wanted to. But try as I might, I rarely got perfect scores in those classes.

And honestly... why was it so important to find the value of X anyway? I was happy to let X just exist without having to worry about its value. I'm not one to judge.

But finding that value was important—because it symbolized how close I could get to perfect. That was the real goal. The actual algebra lesson: how close to 100% can you get, and why didn't you get closer?

In hindsight, my parents never asked, "What happened to the 21%?" when I brought home a 79%. But when I hit that 97%, the focus was always on what was missing—not what was earned.

And when I did earn a 100%, if there was a bonus question—something extra—I'd better go for that, too. Missing it, or worse, not trying, wasn't just a missed opportunity. It felt like failure. Like weakness. Like I had let someone down.

That mindset followed me for most of my life. I was always striving—eager to win, anxious to do my best. Victory tasted like sugar on my tongue. But anything short of first place? That was bitter, and I drank it often, no matter how well I'd done.

I hyper-focused on the falls. The stumbles. The almosts. The not-quites.

I could've multiplied the integers better.
I should've known when Texas became a state. (In case you're wondering—it was 1845.)

And to this day, I will never forget that the word "separate" is spelled with two "e"s, not three. (Not "seperate.")

That 3% even crept into my motherhood.
I couldn't fully celebrate my kids' healthy smiles if one tiny tooth had a small cavity.
I couldn't help but notice when my son misspelled—

*See? Even now, I catch myself doing it.*

Then one day, someone praised me—for the 97%.

"You did so well here," they said. "Consider changing this, but otherwise—you did really well."

And just like that, the lens began to shift.
I am doing things right.
In fact, I'm doing most things right.

It's still an odd feeling. It's not a habit yet. But it's a longing now. A desire. A practice I'm learning.

I am NOT defined by the 3%.
I am defined by the courage to keep going.
By the commitment to show up again and again.
By the decision to grow, even if it's just 1% better than yesterday.

Awesome Annë is measured by the effort.
By the try.
By the rising after the face-plant.
By the grace after the stumble.

Awesome Annë is 97% awesome—and becoming more unstoppable with every breath.

## Their Standalone Moment

Meera opened the door to the hotel room and was surprised to find Omari standing in the hallway. She knew he was coming; she had anticipated his arrival. Yet, her eyes lit up with wonder as she saw him there, as if his presence alone could still take her breath away.

She stepped aside to let him enter, her heart racing with a mix of excitement and nervousness. Her fingers tingled with the urge to reach out and touch him, but she pressed her hands into her pockets, resisting the pull.

Omari walked in, his posture relaxed but confident, his chin slightly elevated as if he owned the space. The door clicked shut behind him, and Meera bolted it before turning to face him.

The air between them was thick with longing, both familiar and new.

She never meant to fall in love again. She never meant to fall in love so easily.

Yet here she was, standing in front of him. She loved him so deeply it scared her.

He reached out, grabbing her wrist with one hand, while his other arm slid around her waist, pulling her toward him. He knew why she hesitated.

And so, their love began again.

## The Red Brick Wall & The Weeping Willow

*Note to self & note to reader:*
*I am not ashamed of my past. What happened to me was not my fault. What happened to me was not my friend's fault. It is okay to share my story.*

I think I was about 8 years old. . . Maybe 9 or 10. I don't remember much, but here's what I do remember.

Back then, every weekend was a church weekend. Saturdays were marked with a prayer meeting in the evening at someone's home, and Sundays began at the church.

On one particularly warm summer Saturday evening, we drove to my friend's home. After the service of songs, testimonies, and prayers, the kids all gathered in the primary bedroom of the church member's home. The grown-ups were separated into two sections - the men sat around on the couches in the living room, some on the floor, others on chairs pulled in from the dining room. The women congregated in the kitchen and family room and gossiped about whose daughter earned valedictorian and whose son was engaged to be married.

And the kids found refuge in the primary bedroom. Some bounced on the edge of the big bed, giggling at silly jokes. Some lay on the floor and watched my brother and his friend play and wrestle. A few girls and I sat together on the other corner of the room, cutting paper into shapes, glueing them into a notebook, and scribbling notes about silly things. We dug through a dented cookie tin of broken crayons, coloring and chattering away.

Maya* (name has been changed to protect the innocent) noticed we were running out of paper. She asked me to go to her room to get more. With a skip in my step, I traipsed to the door of the bedroom, and I peered around the corner to all the grownups in the living room. The lyrical sounds of malayalam conversations filled the air. I straightened up, walked through the living room to the other end of the house where the other bedrooms were lined down a hallway. The left side of the hallway held the doors to the bedrooms. The right side was a wall of red bricks that displayed neatly hung family pictures.
I skipped to Maya's room and stopped suddenly when the light from the hallway caught the reflection of a man in the room. It was Benny Uncle, the dad of another kid. And he was the pastor's brother-in-law. I was too startled to reach in the room to flick on the light-switch. I started to turn away and go back to the kids, but then my eyes caught the pack of paper on my friend's desk. I can just grab the paper and go, I thought. It's not that far from my reach.

With one foot in the hallway, I stepped forward to lean toward the desk and reach for the paper. In frustration I sighed. It's too far, and I move both feet into the room.

As I stretched to touch the paper, his voice stops me. "Hi, molay. Are you coloring? Do you need more paper? Come here." He took the paper off the desk, and moved it closer to him while taunting me with it. I hesitated. Why is he sitting in the dark? I don't move. He called to me again and held out his hand. I stepped back toward the door, one foot back in the hallway. He leaned forward and suddenly grabbed my wrist and pulled me to him. I try to stay planted where I am, but he's stronger than me. He tightened his grip and pulled me to his lap. I squirmed and tried to pull away, but he hugged me close to him. I flinched at the smell of curry on his breath. His voice changed from authority to a husky whisper.

"You are so beautiful. Your hair is soft." He leaned in and moved closer to my face. He smelled my neck, pressing his nostrils to my skin. I lunged toward the door and tried to pull away. He tightened his grip around my waist, and his voice became angry. "Did you hear me, *molay*? You are beautiful."
I jerked my head away, squirmed, and tried to scoot myself off

his lap. I focused on the door and thought about how I needed to run to it. I think that I can escape but before I can jump, he tightened his grip on me.

Suddenly, his rough, calloused hand grabbed my chin and pulled it to his face. His coarse facial hair scratched my skin, and his chapped lips pressed hard on mine. For a moment he loosened his hold on me. I shoved him away and jumped from his arms. I ran to the door and felt a whoosh behind me as his hand tried and missed to grabbed the back of my dress.

I ran into the hallway and then paused, not sure about the living room of adults - including my father - in front of me or what had just happened behind me. I put my fingers to my mouth and began to wipe my lips, first with my fingers, then with the back of my hand.

The feeling of his scratchy face didn't go away. I wipe harder, faster, yet I couldn't erase that rough feeling. I leaned my forehead on the red brick wall and tears pooled in my eyes and trickled down my cheeks. I pressed my forehead harder into the cold, rough brick. I kept my hand on my mouth and continued to wipe, harder and faster. I could still taste his breath.

I lifted my face and put my lips to the brick and began to rub my mouth on the wall. I could still smell him; I could still feel him. I choked on my sobs and kept rubbing until I tasted blood. The taste of the warm, salty blood took me away from what had just happened. I darted to the bathroom, praying no one would see me and stop me. I locked the door and looked in the mirror. Little cuts around my mouth were red. I washed my face and dried my tears.

It took a few minutes until I was able to leave the bathroom. I didn't realize I went back empty handed until Maya asked why I didn't have the paper. In tears I whispered in her ear what had just happened. "Benny Uncle kissed me in your room."

She looked at me, eyes wide open. She got up to leave. Before I could reach out to grab her hand and stop her from what I knew she was about to do, she was gone. I stumbled behind her, and I watched in the doorway as she walked across the living room of uncles to my dad. She tapped him on his shoulder and whispered in his ear. I saw as she gestured to her room, then to the primary bedroom. His gaze followed her finger, then he looked at me. My eyes darted to my feet, and I shuddered when he sharply called out to my brother and to me that it was time to go home. I still don't know how I managed to move. But I did.

The car ride home was heavy with a thick fog of silence. My mom asked once why my dad was upset. He didn't answer, and she knew not to ask again. When we got home, my brother looked at me with concern in his eyes, and closed the door to his room. Did he know, too?

I went to my room, and I could hear the muffled and angry, hushed voice of my dad as he explained what happened to my mom.

"Annë! Come here!" His voice bellowed down the hall.
I don't remember all that he said to me that night.
I do remember that I was the one who got in trouble that night.
I was spanked for being alone in a dangerous situation.
I was punished and shamed for what happened to me.
I went to bed confused, angry, and sad. Very, very sad.

The next afternoon, when we returned from church, the neighborhood children gathered at our house to play. We started with our usual fierce game of Hide and Seek. On this day, I was determined to find the best hiding spot. The idea of finally winning tasted delicious.

We all gathered in a circle by the garage door behind the house. Our energy was palpable and almost too high to control.

As soon as the red-haired boy from the green house around the corner started counting, we scattered! I darted around the fence, between our house and the neighbor's. As I rounded the corner, I turned around to look behind me, and I walked backward in the direction of the weeping willow. I didn't even realize where I was going until my back hit the trunk, and the vines of the branches fell in front of me.

I leaned back on the sturdy trunk and watched the long vines of the willow tree close like curtains in front of me and then dance around me. Sunlight pierced through the movements of the tender branches and sparkled into my willow tree sanctuary. I closed my eyes and took a deep breath of the earth, and grass, and the tree.

I could hear the sneaky and loud whispers of the red-haired boy as he caught the other kids one by one, and then their chatter as they looked for me. But they didn't know I found this haven. I felt safe, snuggled up inside the weeping willow, hidden from the world.

As their footsteps ran away from the willow to look elsewhere, I sat down at the foot of the trunk and hugged my knees. I was giddy with the idea that I may actually win the game this time.

Suddenly, a wave of relief hit me.

Tears pooled in my eyes and began streaming down my cheeks. The wind lifted some of the vines, and it seemed they were tying to hug me.

It was here that I cried and cried. I finally couldn't feel that man around me.

Here, among the dancing branches, I found comfort and safety.

*Unload your thoughts—just write nonstop for 10 minutes..*

Dearest Adam -

What an absolute blessing it has been to be your mom. Thank you for coming into my life and overwhelming my soul with the sound of your strong voice and passion for life.

Some days I still can't believe that *I* get to be your mom. Who am I to have earned or deserved such an honor?

I have loved you before I even knew you existed within me. I prayed for you, dreamed of you, longed for you. The best joy of my life was the moment I learned I was pregnant. For a few moments, this was my sweet secret, my dream fulfilled.

And then the absolute joy to share with your dad - I can still feel the love and how it fast it grew!

You were the perfect addition to our new family - our firstborn.

Thank you for making me a mother.
Thank you for being the best big brother to your siblings.
Thank you for all the overprotective love you showered on your sisters.
Thank you for being a godly example of a true man of God for your little brother.

You are definitely highly favored in the eyes of our God.

Thank you for being you.

Dearest Jasmine,

Some days I don't know where to begin. You snuck into my world, a fun surprise sibling for Adam. And when we realized I was pregnant again, I was ecstatic. How did I get blessed again so soon after the first?

The outside world tried to plan your arrival, but you came on your own schedule. Again, you almost snuck into the world while the doctor's back was turned. Thank goodness the nurse caught you!

Always observing to learn, quiet and tender hearted, you have been an amazing blessing in my life. Your name was chosen long before you came into my life, and I love that you get to be the namesake for my sister.

Thank you for loving me, especially when I don't deserve it. Thank you for being the best sister and friend to your siblings. It has been one of the greatest joys of my life to see you come into your own.

You may be quiet, but you are fierce and mighty. I will forever be blessed to be called your mom.

Dearest Julia,

How did I get so lucky? Thank you for being the spirit of the family, the voice of reason, and the one who has taught me how to embrace me. You have followed your own beat, your own direction, and while I may have been scared sometimes, you have always proved me wrong.

You are capable. You are smart. You have a tremendous amount of talents and gifts, and I can't believe this blessing I have - *I* get to be your mother!

Thank you for your unwavering convictions, your blossoming compassion for the underdog, and your fierce beliefs and desires to do the right thing.

My world shines brighter every day simply because you are here. I love you more than I can say. Thank you for loving me back!

Dearest Joy,

My calling to be a mother again was the strongest when i prayed for your existence. No other word can describe that feeling when i discovered I was pregnant with you beside ***joy***.

You are here on this earth for a purpose, and I cannot wait to see what our God has in store for you. Your mission started when you were born, and you healed a part of my world that has been broken since your Annette Auntie died.

You are so brave.
You are so smart.
You are kind, loving, and so fierce.

I am blessed beyond words to call you mine.

Dearest Aaron,

You have been an amazing blessing in my life. I cannot even begin to fathom a world without you in it. I thank God every day for giving me you.

**You are the best thing I never knew I always needed.**

Thank you for sharing your talents. Thank you for your unconditional love. And probably one of the most important things of all - thank you for knowing how to make me laugh. That's one of my most favorite things to do on this earth: Laugh with YOU.

*If you could write a letter, who would you write to?
What would you say?*

## Cherish the Mess

*(Note to reader: This was originally published in 2004 through the online Christian magazine, IndaPhatFarm / www.indaphatfarm.com under the title "Childhood." My sweet Adam was 2 years old, and this was my tribute to him. Special thanks to the Editor-in-Chief, Chris George for providing a vehicle to help me always continue writing while raising my children.)*

When I was a kid, I couldn't wait to grow up. I ached for adulthood, thinking that would be the moment I finally got to "live." To me, the adult world looked cool and mysterious—glamorous, even. My parents got to leave the house on their own schedule and drive spaceship-like machines with knobs and buttons. It all seemed so exciting.

Now that I am an adult, I find myself longing for the days of careless freedom. I miss those endless summers when time didn't matter and calendars meant nothing. Saturday mornings meant Froot Loops and Land of the Lost reruns. My brother and I lived for The Banana Splits Show and building forts out of sheets draped over furniture.

It used to make me sad that I couldn't do those things anymore—that skipping housework to go to the park felt irresponsible. But guess what? I found a loophole.

I get to relive my childhood by raising my children. Watching my two-year-old experience life is a gift. I am honored to be the one opening his eyes to the world.

The look on his face as he zipped down a slide for the first time was priceless. His tight grip on my sleeve during his first merry-go-round ride—unforgettable. The sound of his giggles as we hide under the table to surprise Daddy? Sweeter than any music I've ever heard.

He doesn't just glance at the world—he devours it with wonder. His eyes are wide open. He tastes, touches, smells, explores.

He's curious, eager, and undeterred by failure. If something doesn't work the first time, he just tries again.

Because of him, I get to open a brand-new box of crayons and breathe in that waxy kindergarten scent again. I get to build sandcastles, fingerpaint, and stack blocks just to knock them down again. I get to feel the joy of watching him run just to experience the wind against his face.

While I try to teach him life skills, he's been teaching me how to live. In the daily burdens of adulthood, I sometimes forget how beautiful this world is—how much of it feels like a playground crafted by God. We lose our innocence as we age. We get jaded, distracted by money and status. But a fulfilled life doesn't come from wealth—it comes from living.

And thanks to my son, I see that again.

To all the new parents out there: **Cherish every moment**.

The joy of making a mess with your child is always worth the clean-up afterward.

*Take 10 minutes to clear your mind by writing it all out.*

I Stopped Counting

You were once a tiny thing.
Pink and small with fuzz on your head.
I counted your eyes, ears, and nose.
I counted your fingers and your toes.
I counted my one baby.

Some numbers got too big to count.
I loved that I had too many!
I stopped counting the times you made me giggle
No number exists that can say how many times that happened.
And I love that you know how I love to laugh with you.

I stopped counting the pinks,
the purples,
the soft greens, and the bright yellows we found
in our home.
Such joyful hues for my life!

I stopped counting the frills and laces.
I stopped counting the bows - both big and little.
I stopped counting the stuffed animals - oh the number!!

Your menagerie was a highlight, for sure!

We loved Duckie, the giraffe

and Grace, the red panda.

From snakes to miscellaneous monsters,

you had quite the collection.

I stopped counting the falls,

the scrapes,

the bruises,

and the tears.

One broken foot

A big burn on your thigh

Even the kitten scratches that could only be soothed with a Hello

Kitty bandaid.

I stopped counting the heartaches.

No cute character could heal the bullying

the hurtful words

the assaults

the pain

the self harm

the dangerous ideations

the attempts to follow through.

I stopped counting the cuts

I hated that there were so many!

Down one arm and up the other

Deep enough to bleed but not deep enough to stop

Down one leg and up the other

I stopped counting the ambulance rides

I stopped counting the admittance forms

I stopped counting the blood draws

I stopped counting the medications

But I needed to start counting again.

I count the victories.

I count the wins.

I count the breaths you breathed.

I count our laughs.

I count your life.

And my favorite of all -

I count you.

*There's a hope you hold quietly—explore where it comes from, and why you keep it close.*

My Childhood Dream

When I was a little girl,
I dreamed of one day enjoying
the company of an elephant.

I didn't let Daddy's laughter
tease me away from that dream.

I could imagine it—
Powerfully graceful,
Majestic and humble,
With delicate, mighty steps
stomping through tall blades of grass.

Elegant grandeur,
with ancient innocence,
my dear pet would lean into me with
a gentle—but royal—stance,
loving and protective.

A *jhul* of gold thread and blue beads
would drape the back of my elephant—
like a tapestry woven from life, loss, and love:
alike but different, quiet but loud,
sad but happy.

I still see my elephant
in my dreams.

*Recall a time when joy came softly, without fanfare. What did that quiet moment teach you?*

Distance & Space in Three Parts

The Distance Between Us (Her Space): *Your world is rooted. Mine is moving.*

I drive fast—
like I do when I'm speeding to you.
Radio high,
windows down,
my hair dancing around me.

I want to come to you.
I don't want to slow down.

But you're not near me.
You're across state lines,
away in a land I've never seen—
hidden and grounded in a forest.
It's a foreign land to me, a strange place.
And so real to you.

I look up as I race the lights.
The moon hangs above the city haze.
Are you looking at it too?
Do you see it through the trees?

I hear the wind whispering your name.
Can you hear my heartbeat?

I want to be in that place with you.
I want to see that place I've never seen.
I want to stand where you stand.
I want to feel that forest wind in my hair,
I want to feel that ground beneath my feet,
I want to feel the fire you built warming my skin.

I want.
I want to be close to you.

The Distance Between Us (His Space): *I am rooted. You are moving.*

I hear the engine hum.
The radio high, somewhere far away.
The wind carries your laughter—
or is this just my memory?

I feel you.
I feel you pressing toward me.
I feel you moving closer.
But I stay in my forest, among the trees that have always known me.
I wonder if your world will ever slow down enough to see me.
I wonder if I can keep up with a heart that moves faster than my own.

Curiosity pulls at me and I want to reach for you.
To feel what you feel.
To match the fire you carry in your heart.
I built a fire here.
Its warmth steady, real.
I imagine it mirrors yours—
both of us burning, separate but alive.

I see the moon through the canopy.
I imagine it lights your path too.
Do you feel me here?
Do you hear my heartbeat as I hear yours?

I want to step out of this rooted place.
I want to reach across the space I've built.
I want to touch what you chase.
I want to trust this.
To trust you.

But doubt lingers.
The forest is safe.
The world outside feels uncertain.
I am here.
And I am curious.

The Distance Between Them (The Space Between)

I am the wind that bends the trees,
the whisper slipping through her hair,
the heat of the fire that warms two hearts apart.

I watch her speed across the highway,
windows down, hair flying,
heart chasing a place she cannot reach.

I hear him rooted in the forest,
curious, cautious, fire steady in his hands.

I hold the space between them.
I am the moonlight touching both worlds,
the hush of leaves,
the pulse of night.

I carry their longing,
their hope,
their doubt.

I bend with the motion of her heart,
I steady with the stillness of his.
I am not them,
but I know them.
I feel them reaching.
I feel them burning.

I am always here,
between them,
holding the distance
so that one day,

Maybe they might meet within it.

## Acknowledgements

So many people have poured love, support, and encouragement into this journey, and I am deeply grateful for each of them.

Grace Miller — my dearest friend, the one I love the most — your presence in my life is a gift. Molly MacPherson, thank you for shining the brightest spotlights on my 97%, for helping me learn from the 3%, and, most of all, for teaching me to love myself again.

Melissa Dyess and the team at Missing Piece Solutions — thank you! Your editing and behind-the-scenes magic made this project shine. To my dear friend Danae Burns, thank you for always being a sounding board for my crazy ideas. Abie Gabor, thank you for being my confidant and friend when I most needed the support. And to Jouleen Dering, thank you for loving me through it all.

To Adam, my fierce firstborn; Jasmine, my fragrant flower and sushi connoisseur; Julia, my sunshine I cherish; Joy, my reason for finding life again; and Aaron, my love who is the best gift from heaven—you five are the priceless works of art in my life, my greatest joys, the most important lives I have ever been blessed to love.

Alvin, your sage advice has been a guiding light, and Abe, your brotherly love is something I cherish. Mom and Dad, thank you for loving me, for helping me find Christ, and for teaching me to cling to Him.

To my incredible nieces and nephews—Isaiah, Max, Emmi, Samuel, Addie, Morrison, Jackson, Teddy, and Little Lydia—your fist bumps, hugs, and belly-aching laughs bring me endless joy.

And to everyone who has touched my life, inspired my words, and believed in me—this book carries pieces of you, too.

*"I now see how owning our story and loving ourselves through that process is the bravest thing that we will ever do."*

*- Brené Brown*

Dear Annette,

I still miss you. You will forever be my 16-month-old baby sister. Every single moment of my life I miss you.
Thank you for being the guardian angel for your nieces and nephews.

I will love you always. Give Daddy a hug for me, and tell him I'm still determined in life.

Annë

Made in the USA
Coppell, TX
19 January 2026

68580467R10085